THE GRAPHIC NOVEL
William Shakespeare

PLAIN TEXT VERSION

Script Adaptation: John McDonald
Character Designs & Original Artwork: Jon Haward
Coloring & Lettering: Nigel Dobbyn
Inking Assistant: Gary Erskine

American English Adaptation: Joe Sutliff Sanders
Design & Layout: Jo Wheeler & Greg Powell
Publishing Assistant: Joanna Watts
Additional Information: Karen Wenborn

Editor in Chief: Clive Bryant

Macbeth: The Graphic Novel
Plain Text Version

William Shakespeare

First published: November 2008
Reprinted: May 2011, January 2014, August 2017, November 2020, October 2021, May 2023

Published by: Classical Comics Ltd
Copyright ©2008 Classical Comics Ltd.

Acknowledgments: Every effort has been made to trace copyright holders of
material reproduced in this book. Any rights not acknowledged here will be
acknowledged in subsequent editions if notice is given to Classical Comics Ltd.

Images on pages 3 & 6 reproduced with the kind permission of
the Trustees of the National Library of Scotland. © National Library of Scotland.
Images on page 141 reproduced with the kind permission of The Shakespeare Birthplace Trust.

All enquiries should be addressed to:
Classical Comics Ltd.
PO Box 177
LUDLOW
SY8 9DL
United Kingdom

info@classicalcomics.com
www.classicalcomics.com

ISBN: 978-1-906332-45-7

This book is printed by Graphy Cems, Spain using environmentally safe inks, on paper
from responsible sources. This material can be disposed of by recycling,
incineration for energy recovery, composting and biodegradation.

The rights of John McDonald, Jon Haward, Nigel Dobbyn and Gary Erskine
to be identified as the artists of this work have been asserted in accordance with
the Copyright, Designs and Patents Act 1988 sections 77 and 78.

Contents

Dramatis Personæ

Duncan
King of Scotland

Malcolm
Son of Duncan

Donalbain
Son of Duncan

Macduff
Nobleman of Scotland

Lenox
Nobleman of Scotland

Rosse
Nobleman of Scotland

Lady Macbeth
Wife of Macbeth

Lady Macduff
Wife of Macduff

Siward *Earl of Northumberland,
General of the English forces*

A Gentlewoman attending
to Lady Macbeth

Seyton
An officer serving Macbeth

An English Doctor

A Scottish Doctor

A Porter

An Old Man

Murderer 1

Murderer 2

Murderer 3

Dramatis Personæ

Macbeth
General in the King's Army

Banquo
General in the King's Army

The Ghost of Banquo

Menteth
Nobleman of Scotland

Angus
Nobleman of Scotland

Cathness
Nobleman of Scotland

Young Siward
Son of Siward

Fleance
Son of Banquo

Boy
Son of Macduff

Witch 1

Witch 2

Witch 3

and Lords, Ladies,
Officers, Soldiers,
Messengers, Attendants
and Apparitions.

Hecate
The "Queen" Witch

Prologue

Scotland in the year 1040.

King Duncan has ruled the land for six years, ever since the death of his grandfather, Malcolm II. Duncan is a good king, but even under his kind and gentle ruling, Scotland is far from being a settled nation.

For centuries, following the departure of the Romans, the land has been split in two — with bands of Vikings in the north and tribes of Saxons in the south. It's a barbaric land. Both local tribes have strong leaders: men who rely on the strength of their sword arm for honors and often have to fight for their very survival.

But the country is changing. With the reign of King Duncan comes a rare promise of unity amongst the tribes to create a single, Scottish nation ruled by a single Scottish King. However not everyone welcomes this peace. Some chieftains want to maintain their independence and continue to rebel against the King, often joining forces with warriors from other tribes and from other countries such as Ireland and Norway; and there are even some chieftains who would like to claim the title of King of Scotland for themselves.

To defend his crown, and to maintain order in his land, King Duncan commands a powerful army, led by noblemen who are experienced in the ways of war - and the mightiest and most trusted of these noblemen is King Duncan's cousin, the Thane of Glamis, otherwise known as…

…Macbeth.

Act One
Scene One

A deserted, open place...

CRAAAACKKK!!!!

WHEN SHALL WE THREE MEET AGAIN? IN THUNDER, LIGHTNING, OR IN RAIN?

WHEN THE HURLY-BURLY'S DONE, WHEN THE BATTLE'S LOST AND WON.

THAT WILL BE BEFORE THE SET OF SUN.

WHERE THE PLACE?

UPON THE HEATH.

THERE TO MEET WITH MACBETH.

I COME, GRAYMALKIN!

PADDOCK CALLS.

ANON!

FAIR IS FOUL, AND FOUL IS FAIR:

HOVER THROUGH THE FOG AND FILTHY AIR.

8

WHAT A BRAVE COUSIN AND A GREAT MAN!

BUT OUR SUN DIDN'T SHINE FOR LONG. THE STORM BROKE OUT AGAIN AND OUR TRIUMPH WAS *SHORT-LIVED.*

LISTEN TO THIS, KING OF SCOTLAND: -- NO SOONER HAD THE WESTERN ISLANDERS STARTED TO RUN AWAY THAN THE NORWEGIAN COMMANDER BEGAN *ANOTHER* ASSAULT, WITH *REINFORCEMENTS* AND *FRESH WEAPONS.*

DIDN'T THIS *WORRY* OUR CAPTAINS, *MACBETH* AND *BANQUO?*

ONLY AS MUCH AS *SPARROWS* WORRY *EAGLES* OR *HARES* WORRY *LIONS.* I'M TELLING YOU THE TRUTH, THEY WERE LIKE *FIGHTING MACHINES.*

THEY *TORE INTO* THE ENEMY, AS IF THEY WANTED TO COVER THEMSELVES IN *BLOOD* OR CREATE ANOTHER *GOLGOTHA...*

But I'm weak. My *wounds* need attention.

IT'S THE *THANE OF ROSSE.*

GOD SAVE THE KING!

WHERE HAVE YOU *COME* FROM, HONORABLE THANE?

YOUR *WORDS* ARE AS HONORABLE AS YOUR *WOUNDS.*

GO, GET HIM TO A *DOCTOR.*

WHO'S THIS?

AND IN A *HURRY!* HE LOOKS AS IF HE'S SEEN *REMARKABLE THINGS.*

FROM *FIFE,* GREAT KING; WHERE THE *NORWEGIAN BANNERS* HAVE BEEN FLYING FREELY. THE NORWEGIAN KING HIMSELF, ALONG WITH A *HUGE ARMY,* HELPED BY THAT DISLOYAL TRAITOR, *THE THANE OF CAWDOR,* BEGAN A *TERRIBLE ASSAULT.*

THEN *MACBETH* FEARLESSLY CONFRONTED HIM HEAD-ON AND MATCHED HIM BLOW FOR BLOW IN SINGLE COMBAT -- UNTIL HE FINALLY *GAVE IN* -- AND *VICTORY* WAS *OURS.*

GREAT NEWS!

THE NORWEGIAN KING WANTED TO NEGOTIATE *TERMS,* BUT WE WOULDN'T ALLOW HIM TO BURY HIS MEN UNTIL HE PAID US *TEN THOUSAND DOLLARS* AT *SAINT COLME'S INCH.*

THE THANE OF CAWDOR MUST NEVER BE ALLOWED TO TURN AGAINST US AGAIN. GO SEE TO HIS *IMMEDIATE EXECUTION* AND GIVE HIS *TITLE* TO *MACBETH.*

I'LL MAKE SURE IT'S DONE.

WHAT HE HAS *LOST,* NOBLE MACBETH HAS *WON.*

15

WE'LL GO FROM HERE TO *INVERNESS*, SO WE CAN VISIT YOUR *CASTLE* AND BECOME *CLOSER* FRIENDS.

IT WILL BE MY *PLEASURE.* I'LL ACT AS MESSENGER *MYSELF* AND CARRY THE GOOD NEWS TO MY *WIFE.* SO, KINDLY ALLOW ME TO TAKE MY LEAVE.

WHAT AN HONORABLE MAN YOU ARE!

THE *PRINCE OF CUMBERLAND?* THAT COULD *TRIP* ME UP... UNLESS I *JUMP OVER* HIM. STARS, HIDE YOUR FIRE...

AND DON'T LET ANY LIGHT SHINE ON MY DARK AND DEEP *DESIRE.* MY EYES PREFER NOT TO SEE WHAT MY HAND MIGHT DO. NEVERTHELESS... LET IT BE DONE.

IT'S *TRUE*, BANQUO, HE REALLY IS A GREAT MAN, AND I'M *HAPPY* TO SAY SO.

LET'S GO AFTER HIM. HE IS SO *CONSCIENTIOUS*, HE'S RACED ON AHEAD TO PREPARE OUR *WELCOME.*

Act One
Scene Five

At Macbeth's castle, in Inverness, Lady Macbeth receives news from her husband...

"THEY MET ME ON THE DAY OF *VICTORY*; AND I'VE DISCOVERED THEY HAVE *SUPERNATURAL INSIGHT.*

WHEN I TRIED TO QUESTION THEM *FURTHER*, THEY *VANISHED* INTO THIN AIR."

"AND, WHILE I WAS STANDING THERE MESMERIZED, MESSENGERS CAME FROM THE KING, CALLING ME *THANE OF CAWDOR.* THIS IS THE TITLE THE WEIRD SISTERS HAD ONLY JUST *GIVEN* ME, AND THEY ALSO REFERRED TO THE FUTURE WITH *HAIL, KING THAT SHALL BE!*"

"I HAD TO DELIVER THIS NEWS TO YOU, MY DEAREST PARTNER OF GREATNESS, SO YOU WOULDN'T LOSE A SECOND OF PLEASURE THROUGH NOT KNOWING WHAT'S BEEN *PROMISED* TO YOU. HOLD IT TO YOUR *HEART* AND FAREWELL."

YOU *ARE* GLAMIS, AND CAWDOR NOW! AND YOU'LL BECOME WHAT HAS BEEN *PROMISED* TO YOU. I'M AFRAID YOUR NATURE IS TOO FULL OF THE *MILK OF HUMAN KINDNESS* TO DO WHAT'S NECESSARY. YOU WANT TO BE *GREAT* -- YOU'RE *AMBITIOUS* -- YOU JUST LACK THE *RUTHLESSNESS* IT TAKES TO *GET* THERE.

YOU ALWAYS WANT TO ACT *HONORABLY* TO GET WHAT YOU DESIRE. YOU WON'T *DOUBLE-DEAL*, BUT YOU STILL LIKE TO WIN WHICHEVER WAY YOU *CAN.* BUT NOW YOU WANT THE THING THAT CAN ONLY BE ACHIEVED BY CERTAIN POSITIVE ACTIONS... ACTIONS YOU'RE *AFRAID* TO CARRY OUT, RATHER THAN ACTIONS YOU'D *REGRET.*

COME *HOME* TO ME SO I CAN CONVINCE YOU TO SEIZE THE BRILLIANT FUTURE THAT *LUCK AND MAGIC* HAVE PROMISED YOU.

WHAT'S THE NEWS?

THE KING'S COMING HERE TONIGHT.

ARE YOU INSANE? ISN'T YOUR MASTER WITH THE KING? IF IT WAS TRUE, HE'D HAVE GIVEN ME SOME WARNING.

IF YOU PLEASE, IT'S TRUE. OUR THANE IS ON HIS WAY. ONE OF MY COLLEAGUES RODE FASTER THAN HIM. HE ARRIVED SO OUT-OF-BREATH, HE COULD BARELY GIVE ME THE MESSAGE.

LOOK AFTER HIM. HE BRINGS WONDERFUL NEWS.

EVEN THE RAVENS SEEM TO KNOW THAT DUNCAN'S ENTRANCE INTO THIS CASTLE WILL BE FATAL.

SO COME, YOU SPIRITS THAT ARE RESPONSIBLE FOR OUR MORTAL THOUGHTS, TAKE AWAY MY WOMANLY GENTLENESS AND FILL ME FROM HEAD TO TOE WITH THE WORST CRUELTY!

THICKEN MY BLOOD. EXTINGUISH ALL PITY AND ALLOW NO SOFT FEELINGS TO GET IN MY WAY!

WHEREVER YOU'RE HIDING, YOU INVISIBLE AGENTS OF MURDER... TURN THE MILK IN MY BREASTS SOUR!

COME, THICK NIGHT... SHROUD YOURSELF WITH THE BLACKEST SMOKE OF HELL SO MY SHARP KNIFE CAN'T SEE THE WOUND IT MAKES, SO HEAVEN CAN'T PEEP THROUGH THE BLANKET OF DARKNESS TO SHOUT "STOP! STOP!"

21

GREAT THANE OF GLAMIS! DESERVING THANE OF CAWDOR! GREATER THAN *BOTH...* ACCORDING TO PROPHESY!

YOUR *LETTER* HAS TAKEN ME *BEYOND* THE IMMEDIATE PRESENT AND *EVEN NOW* I CAN FEEL THE *FUTURE.*

MY DEAREST LOVE, *DUNCAN'S* COMING HERE TONIGHT.

AND WHEN IS HE LEAVING?

HE INTENDS TO LEAVE *TOMORROW.*

HE'LL NEVER *SEE* TOMORROW! MY THANE, YOUR *FACE* IS LIKE A *BOOK* WHERE *ANYONE* CAN READ WHAT'S IN YOUR HEART. YOU'LL HAVE TO *LIGHTEN UP* TO *MISLEAD* THEM. YOUR *HANDSHAKE* AND YOUR *VOICE,* YOUR *WELCOME,* ALL HAVE TO APPEAR *GENUINE.* YOU'LL HAVE TO LOOK AS INNOCENT AS A *FLOWER...*

...A FLOWER THAT'S HIDING A *SERPENT.* DUNCAN HAS TO BE *WINED AND DINED.* YOU CAN LEAVE THE *REAL* BUSINESS OF THE NIGHT TO *ME...*

...BUSINESS THAT WILL SHAPE THE *REST OF OUR* LIVES.

WE'LL TALK ABOUT IT LATER.

JUST BE *CLEAR* IN YOUR MIND... DON'T *REGRET* THIS CHANCE FOREVER. LEAVE ALL THE REST TO *ME.*

22

STOP! LEAVE ME ALONE! I'M NOT AFRAID TO DO ANYTHING THAT BEFITS A MAN -- BUT ANYONE WHO DARES TO DO MORE THAN THAT IS AN ANIMAL!

SO WHAT ANIMAL MADE YOU BREAK YOUR PROMISE TO ME? WHEN YOU DARED TO DO IT, THEN YOU WERE A MAN. AND, IF YOU WERE KING, YOU'D BE EVEN MORE OF A MAN. TIME AND PLACE DIDN'T MATTER THEN, BUT NOW YOU'RE MAKING EXCUSES.

NOW THERE IS NOTHING BUT EXCUSES AND THAT WILL BE YOUR UNDOING.

I HAVE BREAST FED, AND I KNOW HOW TENDER A THING IT IS TO LOVE THE BABY THAT TAKES MILK FROM ME. BUT I'D RATHER PULL MY NIPPLE FROM HIS GUMS AND BASH HIS BRAINS OUT THAN BREAK A PROMISE I'D MADE TO YOU!

WHAT IF WE FAIL?

THEN WE FAIL! BUT IF YOU KEEP YOUR NERVE, THEN WE WON'T FAIL.

31

A while later...

THE WINE THAT HAS MADE THEM *DRUNK* HAS MADE ME *BRAVE.* IT'S PUT OUT THEIR FLAME, BUT FILLED *ME* WITH *FIRE!*

QUIET!

IT WAS AN *OWL* SHRIEK -- A FATAL *BELLMAN* SAYING A FINAL *GOODNIGHT.* HE'S DOING IT. THE DOORS ARE OPEN AND THE *DRUNKEN ATTENDANTS* ARE *SNORING.* I'VE DRUGGED THEIR DRINKS SO MUCH THEY DON'T CARE WHETHER THEY'RE *ALIVE OR DEAD.*

WHO'S THERE? WHO IS IT?

OH NO! THEY MUST HAVE *WOKEN,* AND IT *HASN'T BEEN DONE.* WE'VE BEEN CAUGHT IN THE ACT -- *LISTEN !* -- I LEFT THE *DAGGERS* READY FOR HIM... HE COULDN'T *MISS* THEM. IF DUNCAN HADN'T LOOKED LIKE MY *FATHER* AS HE SLEPT, I'D HAVE DONE IT *MYSELF.*

MY HUSBAND!

I'VE *DONE* IT. DID YOU HEAR A *NOISE?*

I HEARD AN *OWL* SCREAM AND THE *CRICKETS* CRY. DID YOU NOT *SPEAK?*

33

35

38

WHY SIR, IT MAKES YOUR *NOSE RED*, MAKES YOU *SLEEP* AND MAKES YOU *URINATE*. *LUST* SIR, IT *ENCOURAGES* AND *DISCOURAGES*. IT *ENCOURAGES* THE *DESIRE*, BUT *DISCOURAGES* THE *PERFORMANCE*.

SO, DRINK CAN BE SAID TO BE A *HYPOCRITE* WHEN IT COMES TO *LUST*. IT *MAKES* IT AND *BREAKS* IT. IT TURNS IT *ON* AND TURNS IT *OFF*. IT MAKES IT *STAND UP* AND *LIE DOWN*. IN SHORT, IT *LIES* TO LUST.

I'D SAY THE *DRINK* LIED TO *YOU* LAST NIGHT.

IT CERTAINLY *DID* SIR, THROUGH ITS *TEETH*. BUT I GOT EVEN. I RECKON I WAS *TOO STRONG* FOR IT BECAUSE, EVEN THOUGH IT TOOK MY *LEGS* AWAY, I *THREW IT BACK*.

OUR *KNOCKING* MUST HAVE *DISTURBED* HIM. HERE HE COMES.

GOOD MORNING, NOBLE SIR!

IS YOUR *MASTER* AWAKE?

GOOD MORNING TO YOU BOTH.

IS THE *KING* UP YET, HONORABLE THANE?

NOT YET.

HE ORDERED ME TO CALL HIM *EARLY*. I WAS VERY NEARLY *LATE*.

39

41

43

45

Act Two
Scene Four

Later that day, outside Macbeth's castle, the Thane of Rosse meets with an old man...

GOOD FATHER, YOU CAN SEE THE *HEAVENS* ARE *ANGRY* ABOUT WHAT'S BEEN DONE HERE ON EARTH. THEY TURN *DAY* INTO *NIGHT*. IT SHOULD BE *BRIGHT*, BUT *DARKNESS* COVERS THE SUN. MAYBE THE DAYLIGHT'S *ASHAMED* TO SHOW ITS FACE AND THAT'S WHY IT ALLOWS THE *NIGHT* TO BURY THE EARTH IN *SHADOW*.

I CAN REMEMBER BACK *SEVENTY YEARS* -- AND I'VE SEEN SOME *STRANGE THINGS* IN THAT TIME -- BUT *NOTHING* AS TERRIBLE AS *LAST NIGHT*.

IT'S *UNNATURAL*, JUST LIKE THAT BUSINESS UP THERE. LAST TUESDAY, A HIGH-FLYING *FALCON* WAS HUNTED AND KILLED BY A MOUSING *OWL*.

AND HERE'S SOMETHING *ELSE* THAT'S STRANGE BUT TRUE... DUNCAN'S *HORSES*, THE MOST *PERFECT EXAMPLES OF THEIR BREED*, WENT *WILD* AND BROKE OUT OF THEIR *STALLS*. THEY COULDN'T BE *CONTROLLED* -- IT WAS LIKE THEY WERE *POSSESSED* BY SOME *DEMON* THAT *HATED MANKIND*.

I HEARD THEY *ATE* EACH OTHER.

THEY *DID*. I *SAW* IT WITH MY *OWN EYES*.

HERE COMES *MACDUFF*.

46

47

Act Three
Scene One

Macbeth is now King of Scotland. In the King's Palace at Forres, Banquo is suspicious...

TAN-TARA!

TAN-TARA!

AH, OUR *CHIEF GUEST'S* HERE.

IT WOULD BE *BAD MANNERS* TO *FORGET* HIM -- OUR *GREAT FEAST* WOULDN'T BE COMPLETE *WITHOUT* HIM.

YOU HAVE IT *ALL... KING, CAWDOR, GLAMIS, EVERYTHING.* JUST AS THE *WEIRD WOMEN* PROMISED. BUT, I SUSPECT YOU HAVEN'T PLAYED *FAIR* TO *GET* IT. STILL, THEY SAID IT WON'T *STAY* IN YOUR FAMILY, THAT I'LL BE THE *FATHER* OF *MANY KINGS.* IF THEY TOLD *YOU* THE TRUTH, THEN WHY SHOULDN'T I HOPE THEIR PROPHESIES WILL COME TRUE FOR *ME?*

HUSH; NO MORE!

WE'RE HOLDING A *FORMAL BANQUET* TONIGHT, SIR. AND I'LL EXPECT YOU TO *BE* THERE.

YOUR *COMMANDS* AND *MY DUTIES* ARE LINKED TOGETHER WITH AN *UNBREAKABLE BOND...* FOREVER.

ARE YOU GOING OUT *RIDING* THIS AFTERNOON?

YES, I AM.

I'D HAVE VALUED YOUR *GOOD ADVICE* IN TODAY'S *COUNCIL MEETING;* BUT *TOMORROW* WILL DO. ARE YOU RIDING FAR?

DON'T MISS OUR *BANQUET.*

I *WON'T,* MY LORD.

AS *FAR,* MY LORD, AS I CAN BETWEEN *NOW* AND *SUPPER* -- UNLESS MY *HORSE* LETS ME DOWN, IN WHICH CASE I MIGHT BE BACK AN HOUR OR TWO AFTER NIGHTFALL.

WE HEAR *DUNCAN'S SONS* ARE *HIDING* IN *ENGLAND* AND *IRELAND,* REFUSING TO ADMIT TO THE CRUEL KILLING OF THEIR FATHER. THEY'RE TELLING *OUTRAGEOUS LIES* TO ANYONE WHO'LL LISTEN. BUT MORE ON THAT TOMORROW, WHEN WE GET A CHANCE TO DISCUSS *MATTERS OF STATE* TOGETHER.

GO TO YOUR HORSE. *FAREWELL...* UNTIL TONIGHT.

IS *FLEANCE* GOING WITH YOU?

YES, MY LORD. HE'S *WAITING* FOR ME.

MAY YOUR HORSES BE *SWIFT AND STEADY.* HAVE A SAFE RIDE.

FAREWELL.

ARE THOSE *MEN* HERE?

THEY *ARE*, MY LORD, OUTSIDE THE PALACE GATE.

BRING THEM TO ME.

EVERYONE... USE YOUR TIME AS YOU *PLEASE* UNTIL *SEVEN TONIGHT*. TO BE IN THE BEST FORM FOR SOCIALIZING, WE'LL SPEND THE AFTERNOON *ALONE*. UNTIL THEN, *GOD BE WITH YOU*.

TO BE *KING* IS *NOTHING*. TO *STAY* KING... *THAT'S* WHAT MATTERS. MY FEAR OF *BANQUO* RUNS *DEEP*. IT'S HIS *NATURAL NOBILITY* THAT'S SO THREATENING.

HE'S AFRAID OF *NOTHING*, BUT HE'S ALSO *CLEVER* ENOUGH ONLY TO ACT WHEN THE *TIME'S RIGHT*. HE'S THE ONLY ONE I'M *AFRAID* OF AND, BESIDE HIM, MY *REPUTATION'S DIMINISHED* -- JUST LIKE *MARK ANTONY'S* WAS BY *CAESAR*.

HE *REPROACHED* THE WITCHES WHEN THEY FIRST GAVE ME THE NAME OF "*KING*". HE INSISTED THEY SPEAK TO *HIM*. AND, WHEN THEY *DID*, THEY SAID HE'D BE *FATHER* TO A *LINE OF KINGS*.

51

SO... THEY'VE PUT A *USELESS CROWN* ON MY HEAD AND AN *EMPTY SCEPTER* IN MY HAND. IT WILL ALL BE TAKEN AWAY BY *ANOTHER FAMILY* IF NO SON OF MINE *SUCCEEDS* ME. IF THAT'S THE CASE, I'VE CORRUPTED MY OWN SOUL FOR THE BENEFIT OF *BANQUO'S* DESCENDANTS.

THUMP!!

I'VE MURDERED THE BENEVOLENT DUNCAN FOR *THEM!* I'VE LOST MY PEACE OF MIND FOR *THEM!* JUST FOR *THEM!* I'VE GIVEN MY PRECIOUS SOUL TO THE DEVIL TO MAKE *THEM* KINGS... THE *SONS OF BANQUO KINGS!* I *CAN'T* LET THAT HAPPEN. THERE WILL HAVE TO BE *MORE* KILLING!

WHO'S THERE?

GO TO THE *DOOR* AND STAY THERE 'TIL I *CALL.*

WAS IT *YESTERDAY* WE SPOKE?

IT *WAS,* YOUR HIGHNESS.

WELL THEN, HAVE YOU *THOUGHT* ABOUT WHAT I *SAID?*

52

YOU KNOW YOU WERE KEPT IN POVERTY BY *HIM* AND NOT *ME.*

I TOLD YOU YESTERDAY. I GAVE YOU ALL THE EVIDENCE... HOW YOU WERE *MANIPULATED;* HOW YOU WERE *CHEATED;* HOW IT WAS *DONE* AND WHO *DID* IT; AND EVERYTHING *ELSE* YOU NEEDED TO KNOW. EVEN AN *IDIOT* WOULD SEE THE TRUTH AND REALIZE YOUR PRESENT PREDICAMENT IS THE FAULT OF *BANQUO.*

YOU *TOLD* US.

SO I *DID.* AND I WENT *FURTHER,* WHICH IS THE POINT OF THIS *SECOND MEETING.* ARE YOU SO *FORGIVING* THAT YOU CAN *LET THIS GO?*

ARE YOU SUCH *CHRISTIANS* THAT YOU'D *PRAY* FOR THIS MAN AND HIS CHILDREN? A MAN WHOSE HEAVY HAND HAS *OPPRESSED* YOU AND YOURS, AND KEPT YOU *POOR* FOREVER?

WE *ARE* MEN, MY LIEGE.

YES, IN *DEFINITION* YOU *PASS* FOR MEN; JUST AS *HOUNDS, MONGRELS, SPANIELS, CURS* AND *WOLVES* ALL GO BY THE NAME OF *DOGS.*

A MORE *DETAILED* INTERPRETATION MIGHT DISTINGUISH THE *SLOW* FROM THE *AGILE* AND THE *TAME* FROM THE *HUNTER* AND GIVE EACH OF THEM NATURAL ATTRIBUTES. THAT WAY, THEY'RE RECOGNIZED AS *DISTINCT* FROM EACH OTHER, UNLIKE THE GENERAL DEFINITION THAT LUMPS THEM ALL *TOGETHER.* IT'S THE SAME WITH *MEN...*

53

NOW, IF *YOU* HAVE A PLACE IN THE RECORD BOOKS, ABOVE THE VERY WORST CLASS OF HUMAN, *SAY* IT! AND I'LL PUT SOME *BUSINESS* YOUR WAY THAT'LL TAKE CARE OF YOUR *ENEMY* AND *ENDEAR* YOU TO ME. MY *OWN HEALTH* IS AFFECTED BY HIS LIFE, AND ONLY HIS *DEATH* WILL *CURE* ME.

I'M SO *INCENSED* BY THE WORLD, MY LIEGE, THAT I DON'T CARE *WHAT* I DO TO *SPITE* IT.

I'M THE *SAME*. I'M *SO TIRED* OF *HARDSHIP* AND *BAD LUCK* THAT I'D DO *ANYTHING* TO CHANGE MY LIFE, OR ELSE BE *RID* OF IT.

BOTH OF YOU KNOW THAT *BANQUO* IS YOUR *ENEMY*.

YES, MY LORD.

HE'S MINE *TOO* -- SO MUCH SO THAT EVERY MINUTE HE *LIVES* IS LIKE A *KNIFE-WOUND* IN MY HEART.

I COULD SWEEP HIM AWAY WITH *BRUTE FORCE* IF I WANTED TO, BUT I *MUSTN'T.* WE HAVE SOME *MUTUAL FRIENDS* I DON'T WANT TO *LOSE*. THEY'D BE *OFFENDED* IF I STRUCK HIM DOWN *MYSELF*. THAT'S WHY I'VE COME TO *YOU* FOR HELP. IT HAS TO BE DONE *SECRETLY*, FOR *LOTS* OF REASONS.

WE'LL DO WHATEVER YOU *SAY*, MY LORD.

EVEN THOUGH OUR *LIVES*...

YOUR *COURAGE* IS *OUTSTANDING*.

IN LESS THAN AN HOUR, I'LL ADVISE YOU WHERE TO *LIE IN WAIT*. YOUR *TIMING* HAS TO BE *PERFECT*. IT HAS TO BE DONE *TONIGHT*... AND SOME DISTANCE FROM THE *PALACE*.

REMEMBER, I WANT A *CLEAN JOB*. NO *BUNGLING* OR *BOTCHING*. HIS SON, *FLEANCE*, WILL BE WITH HIM. *HIS* DEATH IS JUST AS IMPORTANT AS HIS *FATHER'S*.

GO AND *PREPARE* YOURSELVES. I'LL COME TO YOU *SHORTLY*.

WE *ARE* PREPARED, MY LORD.

STAY IN THIS *BUILDING*. I'LL CALL FOR YOU *SOON*.

IT'S *DONE*. BANQUO, IF YOU'RE *DESTINED* FOR *HEAVEN*, YOU'LL BE THERE TONIGHT.

55

57

COME ON, DARK NIGHT. COVER UP THE LIGHT OF THIS PITIFUL DAY. TEAR THE LIVES THAT WORRY ME TO PIECES WITH YOUR *BLOODY, HIDDEN HANDS!*

WHAT'S GOING TO BE DONE?

THE LIGHT'S FADING AND THE *CROWS* ARE FLYING OFF TO THEIR *WOODLAND NESTS.* ALL THE NICE, BRIGHT THINGS OF THE DAY ARE BEGINNING TO *FALL ASLEEP...* WHILE NIGHT'S *BLACK, EVIL AGENTS* START TO STALK THEIR *PREY.*

YOU DON'T NEED TO *KNOW,* MY DEAR... UNTIL YOU *CONGRATULATE* ME FOR DOING IT.

YOU DON'T UNDERSTAND WHAT I'M *TALKING* ABOUT, *DO YOU?* BUT JUST *WAIT AND SEE.* WE *STARTED* THIS THING, AND WE'LL *FINISH* IT. SO, PLEASE, COME WITH ME.

61

THERE'S *BLOOD* ON YOUR FACE.

IT'S *BANQUO'S*.

BETTER ON THE OUTSIDE OF *YOU* THAN ON THE *INSIDE* OF *HIM*. IS HE *DEAD*?

HIS *THROAT IS CUT*, MY LORD. I *KILLED* HIM.

THEN YOU'RE THE *BEST* OF CUT-THROATS. BUT WHOEVER DID THE SAME FOR *FLEANCE* IS EVEN *BETTER*. IF YOU DID *THAT*, YOU HAVE *NO EQUAL*.

MOST ROYAL SIR... *FLEANCE ESCAPED*.

THEN... HERE COME MY *DEMONS* AGAIN. JUST WHEN I WAS FEELING *GOOD*; AS STEADY AS *MARBLE*, SOLID AS A *ROCK*, FREE AS THE *AIR*. NOW, SUDDENLY... I FEEL *ENCLOSED, CRAMPED, CONFINED* AND *STIFLED* AGAIN BY *CREEPING DOUBTS* AND *FEARS*.

BUT *BANQUO'S DEAD*?

YES, MY GOOD LORD, DEAD AND BURIED IN A *DITCH*, WITH *TWENTY DEEP GASHES* IN HIS HEAD; *EACH ONE* OF THEM ENOUGH TO *KILL* HIM.

THANK YOU FOR THAT.

63

GET AWAY! GET OUT OF MY SIGHT! GET BACK TO YOUR GRAVE! YOUR BONES HAVE NO MARROW! YOUR BLOOD'S COLD AND THERE'S NO LIFE IN THOSE STARING EYES!

CRASHHHH!!!

JUST THINK OF THIS AS A NORMAL OCCURRENCE, FRIENDS. THAT'S ALL IT IS, APART FROM SPOILING THE OCCASION.

I'LL DO ANYTHING A MAN DARES TO DO. COME AT ME LIKE A BIG RUSSIAN BEAR, OR LIKE A RHINOCEROS, OR EVEN AN ASIAN TIGER... TAKE ANY OTHER SHAPE, AND MY NERVE WILL HOLD. OR COME BACK TO LIFE AND CHALLENGE ME WITH YOUR SWORD.

IF I FLINCH, THEN CALL ME A COWARD.

GET OUT OF HERE, YOU HORRIBLE SHADOW! GET OUT, YOU GRINNING GHOST!

69

IT'S *GONE*... AND I'M A *MAN* AGAIN.

PLEASE, *SIT DOWN.* You've *ruined* the atmosphere and *broken up the banquet* with your *insanity.*

CAN THESE THINGS *HAPPEN,* AS SUDDENLY AS A *SUMMER SHOWER*... AND YOU'RE NOT *AMAZED?* YOU'RE MAKING ME *DOUBT* MY *OWN SENSES,* IF YOU CAN SEE SUCH SIGHTS AND KEEP THE *COLOR* IN YOUR CHEEKS, WHILE *MINE* ARE *BLEACHED WITH FEAR.*

PLEASE, *DON'T SPEAK* TO HIM. HE'S GETTING *WORSE AND WORSE.* QUESTIONS *INFURIATE* HIM. GOODNIGHT TO YOU ALL. DON'T WORRY ABOUT THE *ORDER OF* YOUR *LEAVING,* JUST *GO AT ONCE!*

GOODNIGHT. I HOPE HIS MAJESTY FEELS *BETTER* SOON.

WHAT SIGHTS, MY LORD?

70

GOODNIGHT TO YOU ALL!

IT WILL HAVE *BLOOD*, THEY SAY; *BLOOD* WILL HAVE *BLOOD!* STONES HAVE BEEN KNOWN TO *MOVE*, AND *TREES* TO *SPEAK*.

SORCERERS HAVE USED *MAGPIES*, *CROWS* AND *ROOKS* TO REVEAL *SECRET MURDERS*.

WHAT'S THE *TIME?*

IT'S ALMOST *MORNING*. DOES IT *MATTER?*

WHAT DO YOU THINK OF *MACDUFF'S* REFUSAL TO OBEY MY *COMMAND* AND ATTEND THE *BANQUET?*

DO YOU KNOW *WHY* HE DIDN'T COME?

I JUST HEARD *UNOFFICIALLY*. BUT I'LL FIND OUT FOR *SURE*. I HAVE *SPIES* IN *ALL THEIR HOUSES*.

TOMORROW I'LL GO AND FIND THE *WEIRD SISTERS.* I'LL GET THEM TO TELL ME *MORE.*

I'M *DETERMINED* TO KNOW THE *WORST,* BY ANY MEANS I CAN. I HAVE TO KNOW, FOR MY *OWN GOOD.* I'VE WADED *SO FAR* INTO THIS RIVER OF BLOOD, THAT *GOING BACK* NOW WOULD BE AS DIFFICULT AS TO *GO ON.* THERE ARE SOME THINGS THAT MUST BE DONE VERY SOON, BEFORE I *THINK* TOO MUCH ABOUT THEM.

YOU'RE BADLY IN NEED OF *SLEEP.*

COME, LET'S GO TO BED. THIS STRANGE *SELF-DOUBT* IS JUST A BEGINNER'S *STAGE-FRIGHT.* WE NEED TO GET *USED* TO THIS -- WE'RE *NEW* TO THIS KIND OF *KILLING.*

Act Three

Scene Six

On the battlements of the King's Palace, two Scottish thanes are concerned...

WHEN WE MET BEFORE, I ONLY *HINTED* AT WHAT I WAS THINKING. I SIMPLY MUST *SPEAK MY MIND*. WHAT HAS *HAPPENED* IS VERY *SUSPICIOUS*.

MACBETH WAS SUPPOSED TO HAVE *LOVED* DUNCAN AND, SUDDENLY, DUNCAN'S *DEAD*. BANQUO WAS A *BRAVE MAN* AND HE'S *KILLED* WHILE OUT *WALKING LATE*. IT COULD EVEN BE THAT *FLEANCE* KILLED HIM, BECAUSE HE *RAN AWAY*...

BUT IT DOESN'T MAKE *SENSE*. WHY *SHOULDN'T* MEN WALK LATE IF THEY WANT TO? AND I REFUSE TO BELIEVE THAT *MALCOLM* AND *DONALBAIN* WOULD KILL THEIR OWN *FATHER*. THESE ARE *LIES!*

THEN, REMEMBER HOW *OUTRAGED* MACBETH WAS? HE IMMEDIATELY *KILLED* THE TWO "*CRIMINALS*", WHO WERE *DRUNK* AND *ASLEEP*, IN A *SELF-RIGHTEOUS RAGE*.

WASN'T THAT A *NOBLE* THING TO DO? YES, AND *CLEVER* TOO. OF COURSE, IT WOULD HAVE *ANGERED* US ALL TO HEAR THE MEN *DENY* IT.

I THINK HE'S MANAGED THINGS *QUITE SHREWDLY*. I ALSO THINK THAT, IF HE HAD *DUNCAN'S SONS* IN PRISON – WHICH I HOPE TO HEAVEN HE *NEVER WILL* – THEY'D SOON DISCOVER THE *PENALTY* FOR *KILLING A FATHER*. SO WOULD *FLEANCE*.

ANOTHER THING... I HEAR *MACDUFF'S* IN *DISGRACE* FOR HIS *OUTSPOKEN WORDS* AND BECAUSE HE *REFUSED* TO ATTEND THE TYRANT'S *BANQUET*. DO YOU KNOW WHERE HE *IS?*

DUNCAN'S *ELDEST SON* IS STAYING AT THE *ENGLISH COURT* AS A GUEST OF *KING EDWARD*. MACDUFF HAS GONE THERE AS *WELL*, TO ASK THE *HOLY KING* FOR *SUPPORT* FROM THE *EARL OF NORTHUMBERLAND* AND FROM THE EARL'S SON, *SIWARD*, WHO'S A GREAT SOLDIER.

77

79

80

81

83

84

85

86

WHAT IS YOUR *WILL*, YOUR *GRACE*?

DID YOU SEE THE *WEIRD SISTERS*?

NO, MY LORD.

DIDN'T THEY COME *PAST* YOU?

I SAW *NO ONE*, MY LORD.

I HOPE THE *AIR* THEY *MOVE* THROUGH GETS *INFECTED* AND ANYONE WHO *TRUSTS* THEM IS *DAMNED* TO HELL!

FLED TO ENGLAND?

YES, MY GOOD LORD.

I HEARD THE *GALLOPING OF A HORSE*. WHO CAME *BY*?

SEVERAL *MESSENGERS*, MY LORD, BRINGING NEWS THAT *MACDUFF* HAS FLED TO *ENGLAND*.

I TOOK *TOO LONG* TO KILL HIM. I SHOULD KNOW THAT A THING'S NOT *DONE* UNTIL IT'S *DONE!* FROM NOW ON, I'LL *ACT FIRST* AND *THINK* ABOUT IT *LATER*.

AND *RIGHT NOW* I THINK I SHOULD *SURPRISE* MACDUFF'S *CASTLE, SEIZE* HIS *LANDS* AND *KILL* HIS *WIFE, CHILDREN* AND *ANYONE ELSE* RELATED TO HIM. NO MORE BRAGGING LIKE A FOOL, I'LL DO IT BEFORE MY DETERMINATION *COOLS*. AND *NO MORE VISIONS!*

WHERE *ARE* THESE MESSENGERS? TAKE ME *TO* THEM.

87

...WHEN WE FLOAT ON A SEA OF UNCERTAINTY, NOT KNOWING *TRUTH* FROM *LIES.* I HAVE TO *GO* NOW, BUT I'LL BE BACK *SOON.*

THINGS CAN'T GET ANY *WORSE.* I'M SURE THEY'LL *IMPROVE.* IT WON'T BE LONG UNTIL EVERYTHING IS BACK TO HOW IT WAS *BEFORE.*

BLESS YOU, MY PRETTY COUSIN.

HE'S AN *ORPHAN,* EVEN THOUGH HE HAS A FATHER.

I'LL LOOK A *FOOL* IF I STAY LONGER, BECAUSE I'LL ONLY *CRY* AND *EMBARRASS* YOU. I'LL GO AT ONCE.

YOUR FATHER'S *DEAD,* YOUNG SIR. WHAT WILL YOU DO *NOW?* HOW WILL YOU *SURVIVE?*

LIKE A *BIRD,* MOTHER.

WHAT? BY EATING *WORMS* AND *FLIES?*

I MEAN, BY *ANY WAY I CAN,* LIKE *THEY* DO.

POOR LITTLE *BIRD!* YOU WOULDN'T BE AFRAID OF THE *NETS* AND *PITS* AND *TRAPS.*

WHY *SHOULD* I, MOTHER? *TRAPS* AREN'T SET FOR *SMALL BIRDS* LIKE *ME.*

91

THERE'S NO *DEVIL* AMONGST THE *LEGIONS OF HELL* MORE EVIL THAN *MACBETH.*

A LACK OF SELF-DISCIPLINE IS A *BAD* FAULT. IT'S BROUGHT DOWN *MANY* A KING. BUT DON'T BE AFRAID TO *TAKE BACK* WHAT'S *YOURS.*

YOU COULD HAVE AS *MUCH PLEASURE* AS YOU *WANT* IN *PRIVATE* AND STILL SEEM *PRINCIPLED* IN PUBLIC. WE'VE ENOUGH *WILLING DAMES.* YOU CAN'T BE SO *INSATIABLE* THAT YOU'D GET THROUGH *ALL THE WOMEN* WHO'D BE PREPARED TO GIVE THEMSELVES TO A *KING?*

I *GRANT* YOU, HE'S *BLOODY* AND *BLATANT, GREEDY* AND *LYING, DECEITFUL, AGGRESSIVE, MALICIOUS* AND FULL OF EVERY *SIN* IN THE BOOK; *BUT* THERE'S NO *END* TO MY *LUST. NONE!*

YOUR *WIVES,* YOUR *DAUGHTERS,* YOUR *MOTHERS* AND YOUR *MAIDS,* COULDN'T SATISFY MY *LUST* AND *DESIRE.* I'D ALLOW *NOTHING* TO GET IN MY WAY. NO, IT'S BETTER THAT *MACBETH* SHOULD RULE.

MAYBE, BUT I'M ALSO SO *GREEDY* THAT, IF I WERE KING, I'D TAKE *ALL THE NOBLES' LANDS.*

I'D WANT THIS ONE'S *JEWELS* AND THAT ONE'S *HOUSE* AND, THE MORE I *HAD,* THE MORE I'D *WANT.* I'D EVEN START *FIGHTS* WITH GOOD AND LOYAL SUBJECTS TO *DESTROY* THEM FOR THEIR *WEALTH.*

THIS *GREED* IS BAD. IT'S *WORSE* THAN LUST. AND IT'S BROUGHT MANY OF OUR KINGS TO *GRIEF.* STILL, DON'T WORRY; THE CROWN OF SCOTLAND HAS ENOUGH WEALTH TO *SATISFY* YOU, WITHOUT HAVING TO TAKE FROM *OTHERS.* THESE VICES ARE *ACCEPTABLE,* WHEN WEIGHED AGAINST YOUR *VIRTUES.*

97

MACDUFF! YOUR *HONEST REACTION* HAS *REMOVED* MY SUSPICION AND CONVINCED ME OF YOUR *LOYALTY.*

THAT *DEVIL MACBETH* HAS TRIED TO *TRICK* ME *SEVERAL* TIMES, AND IT'S MADE ME *CAUTIOUS.* BUT *GOD ABOVE* HAS BROUGHT US TOGETHER, AND I'LL AGREE TO BE *GUIDED* BY YOU.

I *WITHDRAW* ALL THE THINGS I SAID ABOUT MYSELF. THAT'S *NOT* HOW I AM.

I'VE NEVER EVEN *BEEN* WITH A *WOMAN*; NEVER *PERJURED* MYSELF; HARDLY EVER *COVETED* WHAT WASN'T *MINE*; NEVER *BROKE MY PROMISE*; WOULDN'T *BETRAY* EVEN *ONE DEVIL* TO *ANOTHER* AND I LOVE THE *TRUTH* AS MUCH AS *LIFE ITSELF.*

THIS IS THE FIRST TIME I'VE EVER *LIED.*

MY *TRUE SELF* IS *YOURS* AND MY *COUNTRY'S* TO *COMMAND.* BEFORE YOU CAME, OLD *SIWARD* WAS READY TO MARCH WITH TEN THOUSAND GOOD SOLDIERS. NOW WE'LL GO *TOGETHER,* AND *VICTORY* WILL BE THE RESULT OF OUR ARGUMENT!

WHY DON'T YOU *SAY* SOMETHING?

YOU HAD ME *CONFUSED* FOR A WHILE. IT'S HARD TO *RECONCILE* THE THINGS YOU'VE JUST SAID.

WAIT A MOMENT.

An English doctor approaches...

WILL THE *KING* BE COMING OUT?

YES, SIR. THERE'S A *LINE* OF *SICK PEOPLE* WAITING FOR HIM TO *CURE* THEM. THEIR DISEASE *DEFEATS* OUR *MEDICINE,* BUT *GOD* HAS GIVEN SUCH *HEALING POWERS* TO HIS *TOUCH,* THAT THEY'RE *CURED IMMEDIATELY.*

THANK YOU, DOCTOR.

99

POOR COUNTRY! IT'S ALMOST *AFRAID* OF ITSELF. IT CAN'T BE CALLED OUR *MOTHER* ANY MORE, JUST OUR *GRAVE*. IT'S A PLACE WHERE ONLY THE *STUPID* SMILE;

WHERE NOBODY TAKES ANY *NOTICE* OF THE *SIGHS* AND *GROANS* AND *SHRIEKS* THAT CAN BE HEARD EVERYWHERE, AND WHERE *VIOLENCE* AND *SORROW* ARE *COMMONPLACE*. NOBODY ASKS WHO THE *FUNERAL BELL* TOLLS FOR ANY MORE, AND *GOOD MEN'S LIVES* ARE SHORTER THAN THE LIVES OF THE *FLOWERS* THEY WEAR IN THEIR *HATS*.

I KNOW IT'S *TRUE*, COUSIN!

WHAT'S THE *LATEST* TRAGEDY?

IF IT'S AN *HOUR* OLD, IT'S ALREADY *STALE*. THERE'S A *NEW* ONE EVERY *MINUTE*.

HOW IS MY *WIFE*?

WHY... SHE'S *WELL*.

AND MY *CHILDREN*?

WELL TOO.

THE TYRANT HASN'T *BOTHERED* THEM?

NO, THEY WERE *FINE*... WHEN I *LEFT* THEM.

YOU'RE HOLDING SOMETHING *BACK*. WHAT *IS* IT?

ON MY WAY HERE, I HEARD *RUMORS* THAT *MANY MEN* ARE READY TO *FIGHT*. THE TYRANT *KNOWS* THIS, BECAUSE HE'S *MASSING HIS FORCES*. *NOW'S* THE *TIME*.

YOUR *PRESENCE* IN *SCOTLAND* WILL TURN MEN INTO *SOLDIERS* -- EVEN THE *WOMEN* WILL FIGHT TO GET RID OF THEIR *HARDSHIP*.

LET THEM TAKE *COMFORT* - WE'RE *ON OUR WAY*. THE GENEROUS *ENGLISH KING* HAS LENT US *SIWARD* AND *TEN THOUSAND MEN*. AND YOU WON'T FIND A MORE *EXPERIENCED* OR *BETTER* SOLDIER *ANYWHERE*.

I WISH I COULD *ANSWER* THAT GOOD NEWS WITH *MORE* OF THE SAME. BUT WHAT I HAVE TO SAY SHOULD ONLY BE HOWLED OUT INTO THE *DESERT AIR*, WHERE IT CANNOT BE *HEARD*.

CONCERNING *WHAT?* THE *GENERAL* SITUATION, OR IS IT SOMETHING MORE *SPECIFIC?*

IT'S *EVERYONE'S* TRAGEDY... BUT MAINLY *YOURS*.

IF IT'S *MINE*, THEN DON'T KEEP IT *FROM* ME. TELL ME *QUICKLY!*

DON'T *HATE* ME FOREVER FOR *BRINGING* YOU THIS NEWS. IT'S THE *WORST NEWS* YOU'LL EVER *HEAR*.

NO... IS IT WHAT I'M *THINKING?*

105

WASH YOUR HANDS AND *PUT ON YOUR NIGHTGOWN.* DON'T LOOK SO *PALE.*

I TELL YOU AGAIN, *BANQUO'S BURIED,* HE *CAN'T* COME OUT OF HIS *GRAVE.*

That too?

TO BED, TO BED. THERE'S SOMEONE KNOCKING AT THE *GATE.* COME, COME, COME, COME... GIVE ME YOUR *HAND.* WHAT'S *DONE* CANNOT BE *UNDONE.*

TO BED, TO BED, TO BED.

WILL SHE GO BACK TO *BED* NOW?

RIGHT AWAY.

THERE ARE *TERRIBLE RUMORS* GOING AROUND. *HEARTLESS CRIMES* CAN CREATE *MADNESS* LIKE THIS, AND *SICK MINDS* TELL THEIR *SECRETS* TO THEIR *PILLOWS.* SHE HAS MORE NEED OF A *PRIEST* THAN A *PHYSICIAN.*

GOD FORGIVE US ALL!

LOOK AFTER HER. REMOVE ANYTHING SHE COULD USE TO *HARM* HERSELF. AND DON'T TAKE YOUR *EYES* OFF HER.

GOODNIGHT. SHE HAS *BAFFLED MY MIND* AND *SURPRISED MY EYES.* I CAN *THINK,* BUT I DARE NOT *SPEAK.*

GOODNIGHT, DOCTOR.

107

109

Act Five
Scene Three

At Dunsinane, Macbeth receives news about the advance of Malcolm's army...

DON'T BRING ME ANY MORE *REPORTS!* I DON'T CARE IF *EVERY SINGLE ONE* OF THEM *DESERTS* ME. *NOTHING* WILL BOTHER ME UNTIL *BIRNAM WOOD* COMES TO *DUNSINANE.* WHAT *DANGER* IS THAT BOY, *MALCOLM?* WASN'T HE *BORN OF A WOMAN?*

THE *SPIRITS* WHO KNOW THE *FUTURE OF THE WORLD* TOLD ME THIS: *"DON'T BE AFRAID,* MACBETH: *NO MAN* THAT'S *BORN OF A WOMAN* WILL EVER *DEFEAT* YOU".*

THEN *DESERT* ME, TREACHEROUS THANES! *JOIN* THE *ENGLISH DEGENERATES!* MY *STRENGTH OF MIND* AND MY *COURAGE* WILL NEVER WEAKEN WITH *DOUBT,* NOR *SHAKE* WITH *FEAR!*

THE *DEVIL* DAMN YOU TO *BURN,* YOU *CREAM-FACED GOOSE!* WHERE DID YOU GET THAT *STUPID LOOK?*

THERE'S *TEN THOUSAND* --

WHAT, *GEESE?*

SOLDIERS, SIR.

110

111

CURE HER!

CAN'T YOU *TREAT* A *SICK MIND?* CAN'T YOU GET RID OF *BAD MEMORIES?* CAN'T YOU *COOL THE BRAIN?* CAN'T YOU USE SOME *REMEDY* TO CLEAN AWAY ALL THE *TROUBLE* FROM INSIDE HER HEART?

ONLY THE *PATIENT* CAN DO THAT FOR *HERSELF.*

THEN THROW YOUR *MEDICINE* TO THE *DOGS!* I WANT *NONE* OF IT.

COME, PUT ON MY *ARMOR.* GIVE ME MY *STAFF OF OFFICE!*

SEYTON, SEND OUT THE HORSEMEN!

DOCTOR, THE THANES *DESERT* ME.

COME SIR, SEND THEM OUT!

Act Five
Scene Four

Malcolm's army has reached Birnam Wood...

IT WON'T BE LONG NOW BEFORE THE *PROPER CONSTITUTION* OF THE COUNTRY IS *RESTORED.*

THERE'S NO DOUBT ABOUT IT.

WHAT'S THE NAME OF THIS *FOREST?*

BIRNAM WOOD.

TELL EVERY SOLDIER TO CUT DOWN A *BRANCH* AND CARRY IT IN *FRONT* OF HIM. *THAT* WAY, WE'LL *HIDE* THE NUMBER OF *MEN* WE HAVE AND *MISLEAD* THE *ENEMY.*

YES, SIR!

I HEAR THE TYRANT'S FEELING *CONFIDENT* AND *STAYING* IN *DUNSINANE.* HE DOESN'T SEEM TO *CARE* IF WE *LAY SIEGE* TO THE CASTLE.

IT'S HIS *ONLY HOPE.* NEARLY EVERYONE HAS *DESERTED* HIM. THE *REMAINING* ONES HAVE BEEN *FORCED* TO STAY, BUT THEIR *HEARTS* AREN'T *IN* IT.

I'VE ALMOST *FORGOTTEN* THE TASTE OF *FEAR*. THERE WAS A TIME WHEN I'D HAVE *SHUDDERED* AT THE SOUND OF SUCH A SHRIEK. MY *SCALP* WOULD HAVE *CRAWLED*, AS IF IT WAS FULL OF *LICE*. BUT I'VE INDULGED IN *SO MUCH HORROR* THAT *NOTHING* CAN *DISTURB* ME ANY MORE.

Moments later...

WHAT WAS THE *REASON* FOR THAT SCREAM?

THE *QUEEN... IS DEAD*, MY LORD.

SHE SHOULD HAVE DIED *ANOTHER* TIME. A *BETTER* TIME.

TOMORROW AND TOMORROW AND TOMORROW... EACH DAY CREEPING SLOWLY AFTER THE ONE *BEFORE...* UNTIL THE *LAST SECOND OF RECORDED TIME.* AND *EVERY DAY* SHOWING *FOOLS* THE WAY TO *DUSTY DEATH.*

A *BRIEF FLICKER OF LIFE*, LIKE A *CANDLE* IN THE *WIND.*

LIFE'S ONLY A *WALKING SHADOW...* A *POOR ACTOR*, WHO GOES THROUGH THE *MOTIONS* OF HIS SMALL PART ON THE GREAT STAGE AND IS NEVER *HEARD* AGAIN. IT'S A STORY TOLD BY AN *IDIOT*, FULL OF *NOISE* AND *PASSION...* AND MEANING *NOTHING.*

119

125

I WISH OUR *MISSING FRIENDS* WERE HERE.

SOME HAD TO DIE. BUT, WHEN I LOOK AROUND, I SEE THIS *GREAT VICTORY* HAS BEEN WON WITHOUT TOO MANY *CASUALTIES.*

MACDUFF IS MISSING, AND SO IS YOUR NOBLE *SON.*

YOUR *SON* HAS PAID A *SOLDIER'S PRICE,* MY LORD. HE WAS SCARCELY A *MAN,* BUT WITH *SKILL* AND *RESOLVE* HE *FOUGHT* AND *DIED* LIKE ONE.

THEN... HE'S *DEAD?*

YES, AND CARRIED OFF THE FIELD. YOUR *SORROW* MUSTN'T BE MEASURED BY HIS *WORTH,* BECAUSE IT WOULD HAVE NO *END.*

WERE HIS *WOUNDS* ON THE *FRONT* OF HIS BODY?

YES, ON THE FRONT.

WELL THEN, HE'S *GOD'S SOLDIER!* IF I HAD AS MANY *SONS* AS I HAVE *HAIRS*, I COULDN'T *WISH* THEM A BETTER DEATH. HIS *TIME* HAD COME.

HE DESERVES *MORE GRIEVING* THAN THAT, AND HE'LL *GET* IT.

NO, HE *DOESN'T*. THEY SAY HE DIED *BRAVELY* AND DID HIS *DUTY*. AND SO, *GOD BE WITH HIM!*

LOOK, HERE COMES *BETTER* NEWS.

HAIL, KING! FOR THAT'S WHAT YOU *ARE*. HERE'S THE *USURPER'S CURSED HEAD*. *FREEDOM* AT LAST! I SEE YOU SURROUNDED BY YOUR KINGDOM'S *FINEST*, ALL THINKING THE WORDS I WANT THEM TO *SHOUT OUT NOW:*

HAIL, KING OF SCOTLAND!

HAIL, KING OF SCOTLAND!

BANG!!!

BANG!!!

BANG!!!

WE'LL *SWIFTLY REWARD* EVERY *ONE* OF YOU. MY *THANES* AND *KINSMEN*, FROM *NOW* ON YOU ARE *EARLS* - THE *FIRST* IN SCOTLAND TO *HAVE* THAT TITLE.

WE MUST ALSO *BRING HOME*, WITHOUT DELAY, OUR *FRIENDS* WHO WENT INTO *EXILE* TO ESCAPE THE ASSASSINATIONS OF THIS *DEAD BUTCHER* AND HIS *FIENDISH QUEEN* WHO, WE HEAR, *KILLED HERSELF*.

William Shakespeare

(c.1564 - 1616 AD)

National Portrait Gallery, London

William Shakespeare is one of the most widely read authors and possibly the best dramatist ever to live. The actual date of his birth is not known, but April 23, 1564 (St George's Day) has traditionally been his accepted birthday, as this was three days before his baptism. He died on the same date in 1616, at the age of fifty-two.

The life of William Shakespeare can be divided into three acts. The first twenty years of his life were spent in Stratford-upon-Avon, where he grew up, went to school, got married and became a father. The next twenty-five years he spent as an actor and playwright in London. He spent his last few years back in Stratford-upon-Avon, where he enjoyed his retirement in moderate wealth gained from his successful years in the theater.

William, the third of eight children, was the eldest son of tradesman John Shakespeare and Mary Arden. His father was later elected mayor of Stratford, which was the highest post a man in civic politics could attain. In sixteenth-century England, William was lucky to survive into adulthood: syphilis, scurvy, smallpox, tuberculosis, typhus and dysentery shortened life expectancy at the time to approximately thirty-five years. The Bubonic Plague took the lives of many and was believed to have been the cause of death for three of William's seven siblings.

Little is known of William's childhood, but he is thought to have attended the local grammar school, where he studied Latin and English Literature. In 1582, at the age of eighteen, William married a local farmer's daughter, Anne Hathaway, who was eight years his senior and three months pregnant. During their marriage they had three children: Susanna, born on May 26, 1583, and twins, Hamnet and Judith, born on February 2, 1585. Hamnet, William's only son, caught Bubonic Plague and died at the age of eleven.

Five years into his marriage, in 1587, William's wife and children stayed in Stratford, while he moved to London. He appeared as an actor at "The Theatre" (England's first permanent theater), and gave public recitals of his own poems; but he quickly became famous for his playwriting. His fame soon spread far and wide. When Queen Elizabeth I died in 1603, the new King James I (who was already King James VI of Scotland) gave royal consent for Shakespeare's acting company, "The Lord Chamberlain's Men" to be called "The King's Men" in return for entertaining the court. This association was to shape a number of plays, such as *Macbeth*, which was written to please the Scottish King.

William Shakespeare is attributed with writing and collaborating on 38 plays, 154 sonnets and 5 poems, in just twenty-three years between 1590 and 1613. No original manuscript exists for any of his plays, making it hard to accurately date any of them.

However, from their contents and reports at the time, it is believed that his first play was *The Taming of the Shrew* and that his last complete work was *Two Noble Kinsmen*, written two years before he died. The cause of his death remains unknown.

He was buried on April 25, 1616, two days after his death, at the Church of the Holy Trinity (the same Church where he had been baptized fifty-two years earlier). His gravestone bears these words, believed to have been written by William himself:-

"Good friend for Jesus sake forbear,
To dig the dust enclosed here!
Blest be the man that spares these stones,
And curst be he that moves my bones"

At the time of his death, William had substantial properties, which he bestowed on his family and associates from the theater. Most went to his eldest daughter, Susanna. Curiously, all he left to his wife Anne was his second-best bed!

William Shakespeare's last direct descendant died in 1670. She was his granddaughter, Elizabeth.

The Real Macbeth

(c.1005 - 1057 AD)

Macbeth is one of Shakespeare's most famous characters. It is a name that's known the whole world over, but many people don't realize that the story is linked to actual historical events — even if those events have been heavily embellished and altered for the sake of entertainment.

Shakespeare obtained his information about the real Macbeth from Raphael Holinshed's book *The Chronicles of England, Scotland and Ireland*, published in 1574 (which Shakespeare used as a primary resource for all of his historical plays). Holinshed himself derived his information from a variety of sources, most notably Andrew of Wyntoun's *Orygynale Cronykil* (Original Chronicle) which traces a history of Scotland from Biblical times, and Hector Boece's

Scotorum Historiae (Scottish History), published in 1526 and translated from Latin into English by John Bellenden in 1535.

Macbeth, or Mac Bethad as he would have been called, was King of Scotland from 1040 to 1057 (although in Shakespeare's play, his reign is made to appear significantly less than seventeen years). The name "Mac Bethad" means "son of

life" and is actually Irish, rather than Scottish, in origin.

Eleventh-century Scotland was a barbaric land where war and ruthless slaughter were a fact of life. Survival depended on having a strong and capable local ruler or chieftain to protect both life and property. Such a leader would provide a strong paternalistic rule, guarding the family, community and land from all enemies.

Some of these enemies could be, and often were, collections of distant family members challenging the current leadership.

A number of local rulers would often unite under the nominal leadership of one "king" to promote their common interests and to wage war on more distant clans. Interestingly, in those times, kings and rulers could name their own successor – it wasn't a privilege that was handed down from parent to eldest child as the English monarchy operates today. However, family linkage tended to be respected, and the title usually passed to a relative of the king, selected as being the one most suitable for immediate rule and not necessarily the natural heir. Understandably, this selection process would have been challenged, especially by those individuals who felt that they had a greater right to become king than the person taking on the title. Such grievances were often dealt with or pre-empted by the murdering of family members judged unsuitable for power, to ensure that the "favorite" won the race.

Macbeth was the son of Findláech mac Ruaidrí (who was a High Steward of Moray) in the north of Scotland, around 1005. His mother's name is unknown, and indeed her own parentage is inaccurately recorded. It is uncertain whether she was the daughter of King Kenneth II or King

Malcolm II. However, that is largely immaterial as whichever man was Macbeth's grandfather would be a strong enough family link for him to make a claim for the throne.

In 1020, Macbeth's father Findláech died. It is thought that he was killed, most probably by his brother Máel Brigté's son Máel Coluim (Malcolm). Findláech's title of High Steward went to his nephew Gille Coemgáin. In 1032, Gille Coemgáin and fifty other people were burned to death as punishment for the murder of Findláech. This act of retribution could well have been carried out by

Macbeth and his allies. Following Gille Coemgáin's death, Macbeth took the title of High Steward of Moray.

It was around this time that he married Gille Coemgáin's widow, Gruoch, and became step-father to her son, Lulach (which explains why Shakespeare has Lady Macbeth talk about motherhood, whereas at no time does Macbeth make any reference to being a father. Moreover, Macduff states that Macbeth has no children in Act IV Scene III (page 102)). Macbeth's marriage to Gruoch was significant, because she was the grand-daughter of Kenneth III. Therefore through their combined ancestors, the marriage ensured that Macbeth had a strong claim to the throne.

Within a very short space of time, Macbeth's rival Gille Coemgáin had not only lost his life, but his title and his widowed wife had gone swiftly to Macbeth.

While Macbeth was a high-ranking lord of Moray, the King at the time was Donnchad mac Crináin (King Duncan I). Duncan succeeded to the throne when his grandfather, King Malcolm II, died at Glamis. It is thought likely that Malcolm had engineered the succession through the tactical assassination of any family members who might have felt they had a stronger claim to the crown.

Given the circumstances, it would have been a sensible course of action for Duncan to make peace with his remaining family, in particular his cousin Thorfinn the Mighty (Earl of Orkney), his cousin Macbeth, and the person closest to his throne in terms of lineage, namely Gruoch, the wife of Macbeth. Duncan appears to have been unsuccessful in uniting the "royal family", and Macbeth pressed his own claim to the throne with the help of that same cousin and ally, Earl Thorfinn of Orkney. He eventually won the crown by slaying Duncan at Bothgowanan near Elgin in 1040.

Macbeth has been judged by history to be a more able king than his predecessor. Under his rule the kingdom became relatively stable and reasonably

prosperous, so much so, that by 1050 he was confident enough to leave the country for a number of months and make a pilgrimage to Rome. At this time he was said to have been so wealthy that he "scattered alms like seed corn". As Wyntoun's *Orygynale Cronykil* says:-
"In pilgrimage þidder he come, And in almus he sew siluer"

All was not peaceful, however, and in 1054 Duncan I's son, Máel Coluim mac Donnchada (Malcolm Canmore, nicknamed "big head"), challenged Macbeth for the throne of Scotland. He did so in alliance with Siward, Earl of Northumbria (who also happened to be the cousin of Duncan's widow) and they took control of much of southern Scotland. Three years later, on August 15, 1057, Macbeth's army was finally defeated at the Battle of Lumphanan, in Aberdeenshire. Macbeth was killed in battle. He is believed to be buried in the graveyard at Saint Oran's Chapel on the Isle of Iona, the last of many Kings of Alba and Dalriada to be laid to

rest there. This site is also supposed to be the final resting place of King Duncan I.

Unlike in Shakespeare's play, the killing of Macbeth didn't result in the crown going straight to Duncan's son Malcolm. It first went to Macbeth's step-son Lulach, on the basis that Kenneth III was his maternal great-grandfather. Lulach was a weak king, and people called him "Lulach the Simple" or "Lulach the Fool". After a few months of rule, he was murdered, and Malcolm, son of Duncan I, became King Malcolm III of Scotland.

No-one knows what happened to Lady Macbeth. Dramatically, Shakespeare has her losing her sanity and taking her own life – however, there is no record of that happening, or even of her falling to a bloody death. Having lived through the murder of her first husband, the killing of her second husband in battle, and the murder of her son, even if she was to outlive them all, it's unlikely that she enjoyed any form of happiness.

Macbeth and the Kings of Scotland

Key:
Parent of ———
Married ═══

"Malcolm I"
King 943-954
Máel Coluim mac Domnaill

"Duff"
King 962-966
Duib mac Máel Coluim

"Kenneth II"
King 971-995
Cináeda mac Máel Coluim

"Kenneth III"
King 997-1005
Cináeda mac Duib

"Malcolm II"
King 1005-1034
Máel Coluim mac Cináeda

Domnall

Ruadri

First wife – name unknown — 1 — Boite mac Cináeda — 2 — Gruoch

Máel Brigté

Mormaer of Moray
Findláech mac Ruaidrí

Donada

Bethoc (eldest)

Máel Coluim

Gille Coemgáin — 1 — "Lady Macbeth" Gruoch ingen Boite — 2 — "Macbeth" King 1040-1057 Mac Bethad

"Duncan I"
King 1034-1040
Donnchad mac Crináin

Suthen

Lulach
King 1057-1058
"The Fool"

"Malcolm III"
King 1058-1093
Máel Coluim mac Donnchada

"Donald III"
King 1093-1097
Domnall Bán

The Macbeth Murder Trail

1020 – Macbeth's father Findláech died – thought to have been killed by his own nephew, Máel Coluim. His title of High Steward went to Máel Coluim's brother, Gille Coemgáin.

1032 – Gille Coemgáin and 50 other people were burned to death as punishment for the killing of Findláech. This may have been carried out by Macbeth and his allies as retribution for killing his father. Macbeth then took Coemgáin's title (that had belonged to Macbeth's father) and took Gille Coemgáin's widow, Gruoch, for his wife. There is also a theory that Gille Coemgáin killed Boite mac Cináeda because he had made his wife the heiress to his estate. As retaliation for this murder, Boite's wife,

Gruoch (the stepmother of the Gruoch that married Gille Coemgáin and later Macbeth), mustered an army to kill Gille Coemgáin.

1040 – Macbeth killed King Duncan I at Bothgowanan.

1050 – Macbeth went on a pilgrimage to Rome.

1054 – Máel Coluim mac Donnchada (Malcolm, son of King Duncan I) staked his claim to the throne and challenged Macbeth in the first of a series of battles.

1057 – Macbeth's army was finally defeated by Malcolm's army at the Battle of Lumphanan. Macbeth was killed in battle. Macbeth's step-son Lulach then became King.

1057 – After only a few months of rule, Malcolm killed Lulach to become King Malcolm III of Scotland.

The History of Shakespeare's Macbeth

When comparing the play to the actual historical events, it is clear that those events were merely inspiration for Shakespeare's own take on the story. It is unlikely that he deliberately intended to misrepresent the facts; however, it is important to recognize that as a playwright, Shakespeare had a responsibility to entertain his audience with his works. Therefore, what takes place on the stage is an artistic modification of what took place in history; to give the best portrayal of the plots and motives of the characters in order to arrive at a worthy spectacle. Among other things, Shakespeare possessed good business sense — and a successful play would draw in the fee-paying public to provide him and his troupe with an income.

But money was not his sole concern. His position in society was paramount, and of prime importance was the need to pander to the monarch.

Macbeth is thought to have been written to be performed in honor of a royal visit by the King of Denmark to King James I in 1606. King James I became King of England in 1603 when Elizabeth I died. He was already King of Scotland (King James VI of Scotland). Interestingly, James I was a keen scholar and had such a deep interest in witchcraft that in 1597 he wrote a book on the subject, which he called *Daemonologie*. In it he advocated severe punishment for witches. In addition, he was a keen supporter of the arts, having the title of "The King's Men" bestowed upon Shakespeare's acting company soon after his coronation. In return, The King's Men were expected to perform at court whenever they were asked, which amounted to around a dozen performances each year.

Setting the play in Scotland and including elements of witchcraft appears to be a deliberate attempt by Shakespeare to please the new King. But he can't take the credit for including witchcraft in the tale of *Macbeth*: we have Holinshed to thank for that. Raphael Holinshed's *Chronicles of England, Scotland and Ireland*, first published in 1574, was a primary source of reference for a number of Shakespeare's plays, and *Macbeth* is no exception. The following extract from Holinshed's *Chronicles* demonstrates just how closely Shakespeare borrowed from his version of events:

"It fortuned as Makbeth and Banquho iournied towards Fores, where the king then laie, they went sporting by the waie togither without other company saue onelie themselues, passing thorough the woods and fields, when suddenlie in the middest of a laund, there met them three women in strange and wild apparell, resembling creatures of the elder world, whome when they attentiuelie beheld, woondering much at the sight, the first of them spake and said: All haile Makbeth, thane of Glammis (for he had latelie entered into that dignitie and office by the death of his father Sinell). The second of them said: Haile Makbeth thane of Cawder. But the third said: All haile Makbeth that heereafter shalt be king of Scotland.

Then Banquho: What manner of women (saith he) are you, that seeme so little fauourable vnto me, whereas to my fellow heere, besides high offices, ye assigne also the kingdome, appointing foorth nothing for me at all? Yes, (saith the first of them) we promise greater benefits vnto thee, than vnto him, for he shall reigne in deed, but with an vnluckie end: neither shall he leaue anie issue behind him to succeed in his place, where contrarilie thou in deed shalt not reigne at all, but of thee those shall be borne which shall gouern the Scotish kingdome by long order of continuall descent. Herewith the foresaid women vanished immediatlie out of their sight."

In those days, the Stuart Kings of Scotland (King James I was a Stuart) were believed to have descended from Banquo (this is unproven but may have some truth in it). The witches "predicted" a long line of kings, and this is dealt with in the play verbally in Act I Scene III (page 15) and visually in Act IV Scene I (page 85), when Macbeth is shown a large number of kings in a line, all of whom bear a resemblance to Banquo. The "bloodline" is only made possible by Fleance escaping when his father is attacked. Holinshed describes how Walter Steward, the founder of the Stuart royal family who married the daughter of Robert Bruce, was a descendent of Fleance and therefore Banquo. This ancestral connection must have been behind a change that Shakespeare made to Holinshed's accounts, namely that in Holinshed, Banquo was an accomplice in Duncan's murder; to portray an ancestor of the King as murderous would have been rather

foolhardy on Shakespeare's part. Other pandering includes the reference to the English King (Edward the Confessor) having God-given powers to cure "the evil" in Act IV Scene III (page 99), also known as Scrofula. Edward was believed to have that power, and King James I revived the custom of sufferers being "touched" by the monarch as a cure for it.

But it is with his portrayal of the witches where Shakespeare really aimed to please the King. In his book, King James denounced witchcraft absolutely. It was his belief that witches were mostly women who had masculine features such as facial hair. They were in league with the devil, could summon up spirits, and could even curse images of people to control their destiny. These were early days in the understanding of witchcraft, and the very subject was a threat to King James' belief of divine right of kingship. In his world,

witchcraft was a devil-based display of evil that was an ever-present challenge to the sanctity of his God-given rule. It is a general fear of witchcraft, then, that is the possible reason why neither Holinshed nor Shakespeare ever refers to the women as witches. In fact, the elements of witchcraft that exist in the play, particularly the spells and the appearance of Hecate, are now believed to be later additions, made by Thomas Middleton following on from his own play, *The Witch*. The term only appears once, in Act I Scene III (page 12*), and even then it could be an insult being reported by the speaker.

Beyond the belief that it was written for the visit of the King of Denmark in 1606, a number of other elements point towards it being authored in that year. The Porter's ramblings in Act II Scene III (page 38*) make mention of equivocation:

The line "O, come in, equivocator" may refer to the verbal cunning displayed by Father Garnet, one of the Gunpowder Plot conspirators in the trial of 1606. Also that year, a ship called The Tiger returned to England after a terrible two year voyage, and that ship is named in Act I Scene III (page 12*). However, as the first printed version of the play didn't appear until the Folio printing in 1623, the true dating and authenticity of each of the parts of the play are difficult to establish. For certain, a version of the play was first performed at The Globe Theatre in April 1611.

The Scottish Play

Macbeth is steeped in superstition, so much so that actors consider it the height of bad luck to even utter the name, unless they are rehearsing it at the time. Often, people will make references to "The Bard's Play" or "The Scottish Play" simply to avoid saying the "M"-word. There are a number of theories about the origins of the "curse" of *Macbeth*:

- It is thought that the witches' incantations are taken from real rituals and are believed to cast actual spells on the players.
- Legend has it that in 1606, Hal Berridge, the boy playing Lady Macbeth (remember that all the parts, male and female, were played by males at the time) died backstage.
- Another gruesome legend reports that in 1672 an actor playing the part of Macbeth substituted a real dagger for the blunt stage one, and actually killed the actor playing King Duncan in full view of the audience.

The more rational explanations are easier to accept.

- The majority of the play takes place in darkly lit scenes, and this tended to lead to a lot of accidents backstage.
- Because *Macbeth* is a short play, and so well known, theater groups would perform the play when they were in some financial trouble. Of course, a single play is rarely enough to save an ailing company, and therefore the performance of *Macbeth* became associated with failure, misery, and being out of work.

Whether any of those reasons are true or not is open to much speculation; what is beyond any doubt is that the story of *Macbeth* is a powerful, timeless tale of ambition, of the evil that is embedded in ill-gotten gains, and a question that lies at the heart of life itself — are we all the subjects of fate and destiny? Or do we carve out our own existence on this planet?

Page Creation

In order to create three versions of the same book, the play is first adapted into three scripts: Original Text, Plain Text and Quick Text. While the degree of complexity changes for the dialogue in each script, the artwork remains the same for all three books.

On the left is a rough thumbnail sketch of page 73 created from the script (below). Once the rough sketch is approved, it is redrawn as a clean finished pencil sketch (right).

ACT 3 – SCENE 5

249. Somewhere far beyond the light of the sun, the three Witches huddle. Strange weather and strange landscapes surround them. They sense the approach of Hecate, the Queen of Darkness and they're frightened.

250. BIG. Suddenly she's there! Hecate appears as a triple goddess, with three heads (women's in this frame, all identical, harsh-looking, but not ugly) and three bodies, standing back-to-back. She towers over the three Witches, piercing the gloom with her fierce stare. They cringe and make frightened animal noises.

	QUICK TEXT	PLAIN ENGLISH TEXT	ORIGINAL TEXT
WITCHES (2 & 3)	WHIMPER! WHINE!	WHIMPER! WHINE!	WHIMPER! WHINE!
1ST WITCH	Hecate…you look angry.	Hecate! You look so angry.	Why, how now, Hecate! you look angerly.
HECATE	I am! You dared to meddle with Macbeth In riddles and affairs of death	Have I not reason, chaos that you are, Impertinent and rash? How did you dare To trade and traffic with Macbeth, In riddles, and affairs of death;	Have I not reason, beldams as you are, Saucy, and overbold? How did you dare To trade and traffic with Macbeth, In riddles, and affairs of death;

251. BIGish. The Witches scuttle round Hecate like dogs round their master. Hecate's three heads metamorphose into the heads of a horse, a dog and a boar.

HECATE	You did it without me! And now I clearly see That all you've managed to do Is use him as he has used you.	And I, the mistress of your charms, The true instrument of all harms, Was never called to play my part, Or show the glory of our art? And, which is worse, all you have done Was only for a wayward son, Spiteful, and hateful; who, as others do, Wants all he can get and nought for you.	And I, the mistress of your charms, The close contriver of all harms, Was never call'd to bear my part, Or show the glory of our art? And, which is worse, all you have done Hath been but for a wayward son, Spiteful, and wrathful; who, as others do, Loves for his own ends, not for you.

From the pencil sketch, an inked version of the same page is created (right).

Inking is not simply tracing over the pencil sketch; it is the process of using black ink to fill in the shaded areas and to add clarity, cohesion, depth and texture to the "pencils".

The "inks" give us the final outline, which is checked for accuracy before being passed on to the colorist.

Adding color brings the page and its characters to life.

Each character has a detailed Character Study. This is useful for the artists to refer to and ensures continuity throughout the book.

Macbeth character study

The last stage of page creation is to add the speech bubbles and any sound effects.

Speech bubbles are created from the words in the script and are laid over the finished, colored artwork.

Three versions of lettering are produced for the three different versions of *Macbeth*. These are then saved as final artwork pages and compiled into separate books for printing.

Original Text

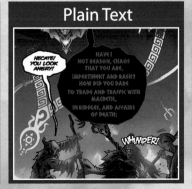

Plain Text

Quick Text

Shakespeare Around the Globe

The Globe Theatre and Shakespeare

It is hard to appreciate today how theaters were actually a new idea in William Shakespeare's time. The very first theater in Elizabethan London to show only plays, aptly called "The Theatre," was introduced by an entrepreneur by the name of James Burbage. In fact, "The Globe Theatre," possibly the most famous theater of that era, was built from the timbers of "The Theatre." The landlord of "The Theatre" was Giles Allen, a Puritan who disapproved of theatrical entertainment. When he decided to enforce a huge rent increase in the winter of 1598, the theater members dismantled the building piece by piece and shipped it across the Thames to Southwark for reassembly. Allen was powerless to do anything, as the company owned the wood - although he spent three years in court trying to sue the perpetrators!

The report of the dismantling party (written by Schoenbaum)

says: "ryotous... armed... with divers and manye unlawfull and offensive weapons... in verye ryotous outragious and forcyble manner and contrarye to the lawes of your highnes Realme... and there pulling breaking and throwing downe the sayd Theater in verye outragious violent and riotous sort to the great disturbance and terrefyeing not onlye of your subjectes... but of divers others of your majesties loving subjectes there neere inhabitinge."

William Shakespeare became a part owner of this new Globe Theatre in 1599. It was one of four major theaters in the area, along with the Swan, the Rose, and the Hope. The exact physical structure of the Globe is unknown, although scholars are fairly sure of some details through drawings from the period. The theater itself was a closed structure with an open courtyard where the stage stood. Tiered galleries around the open area accommodated the wealthier patrons who could afford seats, and those of the lower classes - the "groundlings" - stood around the platform or "thrust" stage during the performance of a play. The space under and behind the stage was used for special effects, storage and costume changes. Surprisingly, although the entire structure was not very big by modern standards, it is known to have accommodated fairly large crowds - as many as 3,000 people - during a single performance.

The Globe II

In 1613, the original Globe Theatre burned to the ground when a cannon shot during a performance of *Henry VIII* set fire to the thatched roof of the gallery. Undeterred, the company completed a new Globe (this time with a tiled roof) on the foundations of its predecessor. Shakespeare didn't write any new plays for this theater. He retired to Stratford-Upon-Avon that year, and died two years later. Performances continued until 1642, when the Puritans closed down all theaters and places of entertainment. Two years later, the Puritans razed the building to the ground in order to build tenements upon the site. No more was to be seen of the Globe for 352 years.

Shakespeare's Globe

Led by the vision of the late Sam Wanamaker, work began on the construction of a new Globe in 1993, close to the site of the original theater. It was completed three years later, and Queen Elizabeth II officially opened the New Globe Theatre on June 12th 1997 with a production of *Henry V.*

The New Globe Theatre is as faithful a reproduction as possible to the Elizabethan theater, given that the details of the original are only known from sketches of the time. The building can accommodate 1,500 people between the galleries and the "groundlings."

www.shakespeares-globe.org

Shakespeare Birthplace Trust

A s so few relics survive from Shakespeare's life, it is amazing that the house where he was born and raised remains intact. It is owned and cared for by the Shakespeare Birthplace Trust, which looks after a number of houses in the area:

Shakespeare's Birthplace

- Shakespeare's Birthplace.
- Mary Arden's Farm: The childhood home of Shakespeare's mother.
- Anne Hathaway's Cottage: The childhood home of Shakespeare's wife.
- Hall's Croft: The home of Shakespeare's eldest daughter, Susanna.
- New Place: Only the grounds exist of the house where Shakespeare died in 1616.
- Nash's House: The home of Shakespeare's granddaughter.

www.shakespeare.org.uk

Martin Droeshout's engraving of Shakespeare

Formed in 1847, the Trust also works to promote Shakespeare around the world. In early 2009, it announced that it had found a new Shakespeare portrait, believed to have been painted within his lifetime, with a trail of provenance that links it to Shakespeare himself.

It is accepted that Martin Droeshout's engraving (left) that appears on the First Folio of 1623 is an authentic likeness of Shakespeare because the people involved in its publication would have personally known him. This new portrait (once owned by Henry Wriothesley, 3rd Earl of Southampton, one of Shakespeare's most loyal supporters) is so similar in all facial aspects that it is now suspected to have been the source that Droeshout used for his famous engraving. www.shakespearefound.org.uk

MORE TITLES AVAILABLE FROM

Shakespeare's plays in a choice of 3 text versions. Simply choose the text version to match your reading level.

Original Text — SHAKESPEARE'S ENTIRE PLAY AS A FULL COLOR GRAPHIC NOVEL!

Plain Text — THE ENTIRE PLAY TRANSLATED INTO PLAIN ENGLISH!

Quick Text — THE ENTIRE PLAY IN QUICK MODERN ENGLISH FOR A FAST-PACED READ!

Romeo & Juliet: The Graphic Novel (William Shakespeare)

- Script Adaptation: John McDonald • Linework: Will Volley
- Colors: Jim Devlin • Letters: Jim Campbell
- 168 Pages

ISBN: 978-1-906332-61-7 | ISBN: 978-1-906332-62-4 | ISBN: 978-1-906332-63-1

A Midsummer Night's Dream: The Graphic Novel (William Shakespeare)

- Script Adaptation: John McDonald • Characters & Artwork: Kat Nicholson & Jason Cardy
- Letters: Jim Campbell
- 144 Pages

ISBN: 978-1-907127-28-1 | ISBN: 978-1-907127-29-8 | ISBN: 978-1-907127-30-4

The Tempest: The Graphic Novel (William Shakespeare)

- Script Adaptation: John McDonald • Pencils: Jon Haward
- Inks: Gary Erskine • Colors: & Letters: Nigel Dobbyn
- 144 Pages

ISBN: 978-1-906332-69-3 | ISBN: 978-1-906332-70-9 | ISBN: 978-1-906332-71-6

Henry V: The Graphic Novel (William Shakespeare)

- Script Adaptation: John McDonald • Pencils: Neill Cameron • Inks: Bambos
- Colors: Jason Cardy & Kat Nicholson • Letters: Nigel Dobbyn
- 144 Pages

ISBN: 978-1-906332-41-9 | ISBN: 978-1-906332-42-6 | ISBN: 978-1-906332-43-3

AVAILABLE IN THREE TEXT VERSIONS

Macbeth:
The Graphic Novel
Original Text

ISBN:
978-1-906332-44-0

THE ENTIRE PLAY TRANSLATED INTO PLAIN ENGLISH!

Macbeth:
The Graphic Novel
Plain Text

ISBN:
978-1-906332-45-7

THE ENTIRE PLAY IN QUICK MODERN ENGLISH FOR A FAST-PACED READ!

Macbeth:
The Graphic Novel
Quick Text

ISBN:
978-1-906332-46-4

THE ENTIRE SHAKESPEARE PLAY - AS A GRAPHIC NOVEL

CHOOSE FROM ONE OF THREE TEXT VERSIONS, ALL USING THE SAME HIGH QUALITY ARTWORK:

Original Text

This is the full, original script -
just as The Bard intended.
This version is ideal for purists,
students and for readers
who want to experience the
unaltered text: all of the text,
all of the excitement!

Plain Text

We take the original script and
"convert" it into modern
English, verse-for-verse. If you've
ever wanted to appreciate the
works of Shakespeare fully, but
find the original language rather
cryptic, then this is the version
for you!

Quick Text

We take the dialogue and
reduce it to as few words as
possible while retaining the
full essence of the story.
This version allows readers to
enter into and enjoy the
stories quickly.